Presented to

....

From

....

Just Like Jesus Said

Love Your Neighbor

Illustrations by Susan Reagan

Melody Carlson

Broadman & Holman Publishers Nashville, Tennessee

Cover and interior design: Uttley/DouPonce DesignWorks

Published in 2001 by Broadman & Holman Publishers,
Nashville, Tennessee

Scripture quotations are from the New American
Standard Bible, © the Lockman Foundation,
1960, 1962, 1963, 1971, 1972, 1973, 1975, 1977;
used by permission.

A catalog record for this book is available
from the Library of Congress.

ISBN 0-8054-2383-4

1 2 3 4 5   05 04 03 02 01

Love Your Neighbor

I live in a house on Daffodil Lane

Where the kid next door is *really* a pain.

Tim borrowed my bike and bent the front wheel,

Then said to me, "Hey, no big deal."

As if that's not enough, he frightened my cat,

By swinging a big wooden baseball bat.

Just by an inch, he missed Tabby's head,

But what scared me most is what Grandma said.

I complained to my grandma about this weird kid,

I told her in detail every thing that he did.

She listened and smiled and nodded her head,

But I almost croaked when I heard what she said.

She took down her Bible from up on the shelf,

And read: "Love your neighbor as you love yourself."

I said to my grandma, "You've never met *Tim!*

I'd gladly love anyone — but I can't love *him.*"

I waved "bye" to Grandma and went on my way,

I hoped to forget all she had to say.

Loving your neighbor may sound sweet and good,

But not if your neighbor's named *Timothy Wood!*

I wished I could move to an igloo somewhere.

Where my next door neighbor's a big polar bear.

I'd gladly invite the fine fellow for tea.

He could sit by my fire and watch my TV.

We could play checkers, and police 'n' crooks,

Why, I'd even loan him my favorite books.

To be a good neighbor, I'd surely love *him*.

But, please, don't you tell me I gotta love Tim!

And what if I lived far away in the jungle.

In loving my neighbor, I'd surely not bungle,

Even if bunches of wild chimpanzees

Lived right next door, way up high in the trees.

I'd let them go first when we swung on the vine

If they ate my bananas, I'd say, "Hey, that's fine."

For monkeys don't know what good manners are for.

And they couldn't be worse than Tim Wood is, next door.

Or what if I lived on a boat with a sail,

Where my closest neighbor's a great,

big, blue whale?

I'd be just as good and as nice as can be,

I'd sure love my neighbor and hope he loved me.

And, what if the place that I called my home

Was the very same place that the elephants roam?

I'd cut lots of grass and invite them to lunch,

In the lake, I'd pour grape juice to make purple punch.

And if they forgot to say 'thank-you' or 'please,'

Or didn't say 'bless you' if somebody sneezed,

I wouldn't worry, I'd say, "That's all right,"

We'd be friendly neighbors — and we'd never fight.

Or what if I wandered up north on the loose?

Where my nearest neighbor's a long-legged moose?

To be a good neighbor, I'd cook a fine meal

Of moose-friendly food — not such a big deal.

And even if fifty-four moose-friends came too,

I wouldn't be mad or make a to-do.

Because he's my neighbor I'd be nice to him,

And ever so grateful he's nothing like Tim.

I sat on my front porch and dreamed what I'd do,

If I lived in a cave or a big city zoo.

And all I imagined, no matter how grim,

Seemed pretty good — compared to old Tim.

Then I heard an odd noise and I glanced at Tim's place.

And there sat my neighbor with tears on his face.

I watched in surprise, and then I felt bad.

I wondered what made my neighbor so sad?

I stood and I waved and I called out, "Hello!"

Then got off my porch and walked over real slow.

"What's up?" I asked, "Is the world going to end?"

He frowned, then replied, "I don't have *one* friend."

I swallowed real hard and looked down at my shoes,

I pondered, then wondered what I had to lose.

He wasn't an elephant, moose, or a whale,

He couldn't leap trees or swing by his tail.

Then all of a sudden I wanted to see,

If I could love Tim the same way I love me.

I wasn't real sure about what he would think.

He might laugh out loud or make a big stink.

"Well, Tim," I began, "I'd like to be friends,

And get along better and make some amends."

His eyes lit up, as he said, "That's cool!"

And that's when I learned 'the golden rule.'

Now most of the time, Tim and I have a blast.

And I think that our friendship is one that will last.

But sometimes we battle and both get defeated.

That's when I remember how I like to be treated.

And even on days when we just can't agree.

I try to love Tim the same way I love me.

And I keep these words in my heart and my head,

Love your neighbor as yourself: just like Jesus said.

"'You shall love your neighbor as yourself.'"

MATTHEW 22:39